MW01133983

ACKNOWLEDGMENTS

I would like to express my gratitude to the following people who have helped me publish my first two books and now my third, VESTIGE:

Alexandra Davies, my editor who taught me to keep things simple to create suspense.

Tim Lindsay, CEO and founder of Tellwell Publishing, and his wonderful team who have worked tirelessly throughout my three projects.

Jill Rapp, with whom I shared my own personal experiences and who provided me with insight into the spirit world.

My family and dear friends who have encouraged me to keep writing.

Finally, to all the avid readers of fiction who continue to inspire today's authors.

Dedication:

To my family and friends always loving and inspiring.
With love

QUOTE:

"If you can see only what light reveals and hear only what sound announces, then in truth you do not see nor do you hear."

—Kahlil Gibran

PROLOGUE

Ghosts. Do they exist? Some say yes, while others, perhaps more skeptical, deny it.

My name is Olivia Croft and like most, as a child I had hopes, dreams and fears. However, my fears were not ordinary and caused my parents to grow concerned. One day, I met a psychologist whom my parents thought could help. He was kind, gentle in his approach and knowledgeable.

He never learned the true nature of my tormented existence, in part due to my own resistance to trust another with something I didn't understand myself, and partly due to his own focus on clinical psychopathology.

As an adult, by reading much literature on paranormal phenomena, I learned a great deal. This is what really helped me understand the boundaries between the living and the dead.

Researchers of parapsychology state that approximately 42% of adults have reported some form of contact with the dead. Half of these were heard, a smaller number physically touched and a further minority seen in some form.

But what are these specters? Paranormal investigators, psychologists and scientists have tried to explain the presence of ghosts in the realm of the living. Some claim they are hallucinations, while others maintain they are projections of the unconscious mind in an attempt to reconcile unresolved feelings of desire or guilt.

It has also been said that ghosts are telepathic projections, of either the dead or the living, as described in phenomena such as *astral projection*. Whether they are psychic impressions triggered by a victim's strong emotional pain or the result of other documented hypotheses, why do they linger?

Ghost hunters exploring the interface between the living and spirit world note that they can either speak or remain silent. Regardless, it is agreed among those interested in the paranormal that ghosts have a purpose—some to do good, others to do evil.

So, dear reader, now that I've introduced myself, allow me to tell you and the good doctor a story. My story.

CHAPTER ONE

Saturday, 08:00, June 10th 2019

Dr. Maxwell Stein enjoyed the walk from his Manhattan apartment to his modest private rooms in Brooklyn, where he saw his patients. Now in his late fifties and with many years of experience, he was considered by fellow colleagues an expert in the field of child psychology. Max was simply passionate about helping others work through their problems, enabling his patients and their families to move toward a more hopeful existence. With a wife of twenty years and a teenage son of his own, he understood the intricate nature of family dynamics.

Despite being accustomed to working on a Saturday, today there would be no consultations. The plan was to finish his remaining paperwork and sign off the reports Wilma, his secretary of the last few years, had typed. He was looking forward to a two-week restful vacation with his son Sean at the family's holiday cottage in the Hamptons.

Finally reaching his office, he unlocked the door, entered the quiet space and made himself comfortable behind his desk. As he switched on his computer, he noted the time. Wilma was due to arrive any minute.

Max allowed his mind to wander, thinking of his wife Pamela and how excited she had been anticipating the trip to Chile with her best friend. The memory of her smiling as she left for the airport warmed his heart. So, it was him and Sean for the next couple of weeks, until she returned from her travels and would join them for a few days at their holiday home.

A gentle knock on the office door jolted him back to the present. He turned, expecting to see Wilma, but it was not her. Instead, a young well-dressed lady in her twenties stood in the doorway.

"Dr. Stein?" she enquired.

"Yes. Can I help you?" he asked, noting something vaguely familiar about her. Her light brown hair hung loosely around her face, just touching her shoulders. The subtle scent of a floral perfume filled the air. Her complexion was healthy and her light blue intelligent eyes scanned the office as if in search of something familiar. Then, he noted the dimples on her cheeks as she smiled at him. He knew exactly who she was. "Please have a seat, it's been a long time," he remarked.

"Indeed it has, Doc," she replied, moving closer but not accepting his invitation to sit. Max remembered the extremely shy, troubled and frightened ten year old he had met many years earlier. To this very day he was still not entirely sure what the cause of her angst had been, but today she stood before him with an air of mystery and quiet confidence.

"Here, take this," she said, handing Max a light brown leather diary with her name embossed on its side. It was a name well known to those moving in circles of the justice system. Her grandfather had been a prominent judge and Rotarian, with her own father now following in the same footsteps.

Max took the small book, curious about its content. Before he had the chance to ask any of the questions that had immediately flooded his mind, she was at the door, ready to leave. She stopped and turned.

"Oh, before I forget, your sister said that the spare car keys you are looking for have fallen behind your dresser. The cleaning lady accidentally knocked them off."

She smiled and walked out of his office. His only sister had been dead for five years. Max bolted from behind his desk to stop her, but when he reached the street, she was gone.

Returning to his office still dazed, he bumped into Wilma, spilling the coffee she had made for him.

"Dr. Stein, there you go again, always in a hurry," she teased. "Here is the rest of your coffee and today's paper," she said, handing him the items.

Taking them, he thanked her then walked back into his office and closed the door. As he placed the mug and paper on his desk, his attention was drawn back to the diary that lay next to the keyboard. Max sat quietly, contemplating what to do with the little book. Instead of picking it up, he reached for the morning newspaper. As he saw the headline and image underneath, he froze.

"**Tragic Death of Daughter of Prominent New York Judge.**" The face smiling up at him from the front page was one he had seen moments earlier. He scanned the article for the date of the tragedy: June 7th.

The woman who was just in his office moments earlier had been dead for three days. Cold chills ran down Max's spine. How could this be? He had seen her, spoken with her and experienced the aroma of her perfume. She had held the diary, a solid object, and handed it to him!

Max decided to finish what he had set out to do that morning and then head straight home. A lingering wave of sadness and confusion washed over him. One thing remained certain: he needed to read her diary.

CHAPTER TWO

Sean was setting his packed travel bag next to the front door, when he heard it unlock and open.

"Hey, son," Max greeted entering their modest apartment. "I see you're all packed."

"Yeah, can't wait to get some rest. It's been a long year." Sean stated. "I've left you a blueberry Danish, thinking you might want a snack before we head off."

"Thanks, but I'll pass. Give me ten minutes to pack a few things and then we're out of here," Max announced. He wasn't hungry. As a youngster that particular berry had been his favorite, but with time he had become less fond of it. After placing the diary on his bed, he headed for the closet, pulled out a suitcase and began packing. He slid the diary into a side pocket after zipping up and locking the case.

Then, he remembered the spare car keys, knowing that Sean would want to borrow the Jeep.

'Surely they couldn't be on the floor,' Max thought to himself as he looked behind the dresser. Astonished, and as predicted by the mysterious visitor, he found them lying on the dark brown carpet. Somewhat amused, he grabbed them and joined his son, who was patiently waiting for him by the elevator.

****

Max was tired after the drive to their quaint retreat in the Hamptons. It had been passed down from his great-grandfather through generations and now belonged to him. His son Sean helped unload the Jeep, placing their luggage in the spacious foyer. Having noticed that his father had been unusually quiet during the drive, he volunteered to make dinner.

"I'll cook," Sean said, "how does takeout pizza sound?"

Max smiled and just nodded, appreciative of Sean's innate willingness to help and sense of humor, both characteristics he'd inherited from his mother. While they waited for their order to be delivered, Max made himself comfortable in his favorite recliner, opened the diary and began to read.

****

I, Olivia, was born and raised in New Jersey by two very loving parents. My father, Joseph, worked for the District Attorney's office as a criminal lawyer, while my mother Vera, taught at the local primary school. I had an older brother, Carl, who was extremely protective of the mini aquarium located in his bedroom. I was only permitted to observe the goldfish swim around the fake plants and mini castle that decorated their tank for a few minutes a day, and only under his watchful eye.

"They have feelings, too," he would explain, " they don't want to be stared at all the time." Playing with the pet tortoise he called Pongo, was a big 'no- no'. Only Carl was allowed to hold and feed him.

"You'll drop him because you have small hands. I don't want him to be hurt or die!" my brother would state with a certainty, as if predicting the poor reptile's fate.

The idea of fate and death would unsettle most kids his age, but not Carl, who was blessed with an optimistic temperament and an ability to take events in his stride.

My first memory of experiencing the other world, was before I was even cognizant of what had presented itself to me. I was an infant, lying in my bassinette while my mother washed up after breakfast. A younger woman with a gentle expression of longing, leaned over the bassinette, and just watched me. She returned many times, a wispy white form with cool breath that would tickle my small face, making me giggle. Then, every time that my mother would turn her attention to me, the woman would vanish.

Later, as a teenager, hauntings was a hot topic of conversation around our dinner table, especially at Halloween. My mother, blessed with an active imagination, had a gift for telling a good story. Stories about ghosts were her specialty and my brother's favorite. Once, she told a story about a ghost in our home, little knowing how true it was. I learned that our house had belonged to a family that had a daughter who died through complications of giving birth to a healthy baby girl. As our mother told the story, I chose to keep my own story of the woman's visitations secret, knowing that Carl would make fun of me and our parents would dismiss the experience as a dream.

So I went through life aware of another dimension to the one we knew, but not sharing this knowledge with another living soul.

CHAPTER THREE

The next memorable experience happened when I was six years old. Our house was located close to a small forest and not far from our school, allowing us to either ride our bikes or walk the short distance. One afternoon, Carl had band practice and stayed on at school, leaving me to walk home alone. As I neared the field at the edge of the forest, I noticed a small boy about the same age as me, wearing sneakers, jeans and a light red T-shirt. When he smiled, I saw that like myself, he was missing his front teeth. Instantly I felt curious about him.

"Hey, what's your name?" I asked him.

"Jake," he replied.

Before I could say anything else Jake beckoned me to follow him. I hesitated. My instinct to beware of danger kicked in, but the temptation of learning more about the boy was too strong. Still feeling some doubt, I decided to follow him.

"Come, let me show you something really cool," he said enthusiastically as I drew closer. I followed him, slowly at first, then faster as he gained pace, running off into the woods. Suddenly he stopped and turned around. I was still running, trying to catch up with him. All at once the ground disappeared from under my feet and I tumbled into a large

pit. The fall was quick. My body scraped the dirt walls, as gravity pulled me into the depths of the hole, until I reached the bottom landing with a heavy thud.

In desperation, I looked up to see only the light blue sky and brown foliage of the trees.

Hit by a sense of urgency, I called for help. "Jake! Jake!"

The boy appeared at the edge of the pit and looked down at me. He was grinning in the most menacing way, his face contorted, almost unhuman. Laughter echoed from above, filling the pit and my ears. Then, Jake was gone.

Now alone, a deadly silence surrounded me. The forest had gone completely quiet. Not even the rustling of the leaves from the trees above reached me. A sharp burning sensation moved through my body. Looking down, I noted that my arm was severely scratched and I had a gaping wound on my right leg, pooling with fresh blood. Tears filled my small eyes and quietly rolled down my cheeks. A large lump of anguish filled and stuck in my throat, muffling my sobs of despair. A million questions ran through my mind; who would ever find me, why didn't I heed my instincts, what would become of my family, would Carl get into trouble for not walking part of the way with me. I curled up, making myself as small as possible, fighting the cold and fear. My thoughts turned to Jake, about how cunning and cruel he had been. In spite of the fear and sense of hopelessness blanketing me, my anger kicked in. I wanted to survive.

Suddenly the smell of fuel filled my nostrils. Now I was absolutely petrified! I wondered if burning me alive had been part of Jake's vicious plan! Just as I was about to scream for help, a man climbed down into the pit. He was dressed as a *pilot. Now, upon reflection, his uniform was more in keeping with that of a fighter pilot of World War II.*

He said nothing to comfort me, but with his strong arms, he picked me up and climbed back out of the pit. His clothing was made of a rough material and smelled of fuel. Still in shock, I didn't see his face. In truth, I don't remember how I got home, but the next thing I became aware of was my mother hovering over me, inspecting my wounds and repeatedly asking for an explanation.

My account of events was vague. Carl had already returned from band practice and helped my mother get me into the car. "I am taking you to the emergency room," she told me as she backed the family station wagon out of the driveway. As we passed the field at the edge of the forest, I saw him. Jake.

"That's the boy that made me fall," I said to Carl, pointing at Jake. My brother looked at me perplexed.

"Where? I don't see anybody." Then, leaning closer to my mother's ear, he said, "I think she hit her head. Drive faster if you can, Mom."

We arrived at the hospital where we were met by a nice triage nurse called Linda. I gave a brief fabricated account of events to the young doctor cleaning and treating my injuries.

"I am going to have a quick talk to your mom, ok? Stay here and don't worry. Everything is going to be fine," the young medic said reassuringly. Despite the gentle ways of the doctor, I was unable to relax. My small frame was sore and my leg throbbed with a dull pain where it had been stitched. Out of the blue, my olfactory senses awakened. Once again I could smell fuel! The pilot materialized in front of my eyes. Blinking several times and pinching myself, I had to make

sure that it was not a dream or an aftereffect of the small amount of local anesthetic I'd been administered earlier. It was nice to see him, for I wanted to thank him, but after my experience with Jake, I remained wary of his presence. His face was rugged but his dark brown eyes reflected a kindness. I felt sad for him.

"Tom Hicks," he said, handing me an old silver pocket watch. Taking it, I inspected it and noted the initials T.H. inscribed on the back. The hands on its face had stopped, with the large hand pointing to the twelve and the small one to the two. I wondered if this was the hour that time had stopped for Tom Hicks.

****

There was a knock at the front door. Max could hear Sean open it and complete a transaction with the pizza delivery man. Closing the door behind him, he called out, "Dad, dinner is ready!" When Max came into the kitchen, Sean had placed the large box on the kitchen table which he had already set. Together they ate, talking about their plans for the following days. Sean was especially excited about going skydiving with his father. Max had booked the adventure and together with Sean, watched the dangerous but exhilarating features of the extreme sport on YouTube.

"What are you reading?" Sean asked his father, noticing the diary on the kitchen counter.

"Oh just some private journals," Max replied, helping himself to another slice of the delicious pizza.

The experiences Olivia, his former patient, had described so far had left the seasoned psychologist unsettled and curious. Why had she given him the diary? Why now, after so many years? He was eager to find out.

CHAPTER FOUR

It was late. Sean had gone to bed after watching a series of short documentaries about the most dangerous animals on the planet. Max retired to his room where he climbed into bed, looking forward to a good night's sleep. It was not to be. He lay awake.

His mind wandered back to the time Olivia was under his care. She was bright and articulate for a girl of her age. He had been cautious not to probe too intently on what troubled her during their initial sessions of therapy, though he had wondered whether she would ever open up to him completely. The diary had thus far provided him with a small glimpse into the mind of a very young Olivia.

Unable to rest, he switched the bedside lamp on, reached for the book, opened it to where he had left off and once again, began to read.

****

When I was still a child, my therapist had told me that the causes of anxiety were numerous. He was right about that. However, those he listed did not include what I am about to describe. It happened one week into the summer holidays.

My parents were very good friends with the president of the Rotary club and his wife, the Pritchards. My father accepted an invitation to a BBQ at their new home in celebration of Mr. Pritchard's second term as president of the club. The grounds surrounding the mansion were spectacular with its lawns and garden beds manicured to perfection. The house itself had an old Edwardian charm to it, but to me, it looked sinister.

"Come on, quit staring," my brother said, nudging me toward the main entrance, where our parents were being greeted by our hosts. Inside, the main hallway was mostly decorated with carved mahogany, including the banisters of a wide, winding staircase. I found myself drawn to a room to the left, and when I entered I saw it was a lounge room, lavishly furnished with antiques.

There was a large fireplace, and in front of it stood an upholstered high wing chair. I moved closer, unaware that my family had already made their way to the outdoor entertainment area. In the chair sat a man smoking a cigar. He was dressed in a tuxedo with his hair slicked back and parted to one side. I stopped in my tracks, fear urging me to quietly back out of the room without being noticed, but he turned his head and looked straight at me with dark penetrating eyes. I remember being transfixed and frozen by his intense look. The gray smoke from the cigar gently drifted upwards in a spiraling pattern. I could smell it. He just stared at me. My heart pounded hard against my chest wall. Sweat formed on my brow. I wondered if, like a predator in the jungle, he could smell my fear.

Suddenly, someone tugged at my arm. It was my mother.

"Here you are. Come and meet a nice girl your age."

I followed her, not daring to look back at the man in the chair, but felt the hair on the back of my neck stand up as I walked away.

The rest of the afternoon was equally as intense. My mother introduced me to Cindy, who like me was ten and very friendly. During our interactions I kept touching her to make sure she was actually real and not 'something else'. While my brother and some other kids were playing water polo in the pool, Cindy and I sat by its edge, feet dangling in the water, watching and cheering. Out of nowhere a force coming from behind pushed me into the water. Once I had surfaced and gained composure, thinking it must have been one of the other guests playing a prank, I noted that Cindy was just as shocked as I was. Before I could say anything, something gripped my ankle and forcefully tugged me under the water. My body was steadily being pulled to the bottom of the pool, overpowering my efforts to swim to the surface. I felt physically sick, weak and helpless. I could see the legs of the other kids moving beneath the water's surface as they played polo. I reached out to try and grab someone's foot to draw attention, but I was dragged back out of reach. Looking up, I saw a blurry image of the light blue sky and sunlight decorate the heavens. Feeling lightheaded and disorientated, I realized that I could no longer hold my breath. Suddenly, panic spread throughout my body, triggering a surge of adrenaline. I tried to muster the little energy I had for a 'fight and flight response', but no amount of kicking helped. The grip was firm. Able to turn my upper body, I got a glimpse of a man in a formal white suit with what seemed like a stain on his chest. Horrified at the sight I opened my mouth to scream. It seemed in vain. My screams merely echoed through the density of the liquid as did his in response. Suddenly, there was a crash in the water. Large bubbles surrounded me and then my father's hands were pulling me back up to the surface.

"What the hell happened?" he asked, frightened, as others gathered around to help us out of the swimming pool.

"I don't know. I fell in and panicked," I lied, fearful of what may have occurred by relaying the truth. He held me tight, close to his chest. I could feel our hearts pounding in sequence. Carl touched my foot. He saw what others had not noticed: finger impressions around my ankle.

As an adult I decided to do a little of my own research about that particular property. I learned that it had once belonged to a prominent banker whose wife was having an affair with his close associate. The banker shot his associate in the chest, after catching him by the pool in a rendezvous with his wife.

Being a person of prominence with valuable political connections, the crime was logged as an accident. Today I can appreciate that the manifestation was a part of an unresolved sad story. However, I still don't know what the victim thought I could do for him decades after the fact.

The worst part of this particular encounter, was my increasing awareness of the sinister side of the unknown, which was beginning to impact me at an emotional level. The innocence of childhood had clouded my perception and evaluation of the way our universe worked. I didn't understand the nature of the supernatural experience or its purpose, and with time, it made me start to doubt my own sanity. The one thing I understood well, was my own deep feeling of isolation.

Now, as an adult, I ask myself if I could rewind the hands of time, would I do things differently? Would I confide in my therapist? I've already alluded to the fact that he was a good clinician, but no amount of therapy could have made the hauntings stop. There was no doubt in my mind about that. To this very day, however, I remain uncertain as to whether I would have been believed.

CHAPTER FIVE

The next morning, Max got up early. Not entirely awake, he stubbed his toe on the small step that led into the kitchen. "Damn!" he cursed under his breath, not wanting to wake Sean. Looking into the sparsely filled pantry, he made a mental note of groceries needed for the next few days. Then, he prepared his morning coffee using the new Nespresso machine his wife had given to him for Christmas, and drank it quickly. He was about to leave a note for his son when Sean walked into the kitchen.

"Hey Dad, it's early. Where are you going?" he enquired.

"Just going into town to pick up groceries. Need anything?"

"No thanks. I'm planning on meeting up with Terrence to play golf this morning."

"Sure, no problem. Take your mobile phone and have it on silent in case I need to contact you," Max requested as he grabbed his keys and headed out the door.

The small community they belonged to was friendly. If you hoped to bump into someone there were two places at which that was likely to occur—the grocery store or the bank. Max had just finished placing the large paper bags filled with purchased alimentary items into the Jeep, when a familiar voice called out to him.

"Maxwell!" Turning, he saw his good friend Harvey approaching. They had been friends since college where they were known to prefer playing competitive chess and Scrabble late into the night, while others were out partying hard and nursing hangovers.

"Harvey, my man. What's up?"

"You here on vacation with the family?" Harvey asked, shaking Max's hand.

"Just me and Sean. Pam is traveling in Chile and will join us later on."

"Ok, well why don't you both come to dinner tonight? Just a casual BBQ," Harvey suggested.

"Great. Want us to bring anything?" Max asked, knowing that Harvey's wife, Shirley, loved a good ice cream cake.

"Just yourselves. See you around seven."

The two men bid each other farewell and returned to their respective cars. When Max reached home, he saw that Sean had already gone out for the day. After replenishing the pantry and fridge, he settled into a comfortable garden couch and continued to read more from the diary.

CHAPTER SIX

The sun was shining, warming the outdoor area where Max sat. After reading only a few words of the next entry of Olivia's account, he found his mind wandering. A nagging feeling in the pit of his stomach prevented him from concentrating. Getting up from the couch, he wandered back inside the cottage with a sense of unease and free floating anxiety. As if in search of something, he went from room to room, finally stopping in the small library. Immobile, he stared at the book case. Max noticed a photo album protruding slightly from the shelf. 'That's strange,' he thought, 'everything is usually neat and tightly packed.' Suddenly, he felt intensely drawn to the album, but before he could react, it fell off the shelf. He froze. Unsure of what to make of this, he hastily picked it up, and still holding onto it tightly as if to protect it, he sat down at his desk.

Opening the book of photographic memories, he slowly went through each image, reminiscing about his past. The final photo stood out, once again fueling the nagging feeling. The image of him and his cousins posing around a tractor on his Uncle's farm starred back at him. He stopped. Suddenly the last diary entry he had read invaded his mind, about the issue of being believed and validated. This resonated with his inner core. A memory that had been suppressed for so long.

CHAPTER SEVEN

It was summer when it happened. Max and his family had gone to visit their cousins who owned a blueberry farm in Portland, Maine. In comparison to his older sister Cynthia, he was a quiet and introverted eleven-year-old boy. The home their uncle lived in would have been classified in *Architect Digest* as a New England style house. Max recalled its imposing two story structure composed of two large chimneys, a brick façade, a high-pitched dormered roof and elaborate front entry with a portico supported by columns. The kitchen and living area were on the first floor with five large bedrooms on the second floor.

The weather in Maine at that time of year was characteristically hot and humid, resulting in not too infrequent thunderstorms. However bad, the weather never impacted on the family's activities. A game of Monopoly would routinely follow dinner, played well into the late evening. Max's sister seemed to enjoy the banter with their cousins and when able, without being noticed, would pass a few of the fake money bills to her brother, who inevitably would be on a losing streak. On one particular night, the mood among the kids shifted, becoming more somber. Max remembered the atmosphere in the games room charged with a peculiar heaviness.

"Did you enjoy the game tonight?" he asked Cynthia as they got ready for bed.

"Not really," she answered. "Why?"

"I don't know. Everyone seemed to be in a bad mood." Max climbed into one of the twin beds in the room they shared.

"I guess it would be nice to play a different game once in a while," she remarked, switching the bedside lamp off. In truth, their cousin Tim, a teenager with a domineering personality, took it upon himself to map out the evening's games, without consulting his cousins or siblings.

"We're playing Monopoly and that is final," he would command.

"I hope Tim doesn't miss his calling of becoming a General in the army," Max said half-jokingly, settling under the covers.

Tired and relieved to be on their own, Max and Cynthia both fell into a deep sleep. Outside, the wind howled through the trees and the rain fell in torrents from the dark and almost purple sky, hammering down onto the roof. Then, thunder and lightning followed. A full-blown storm had developed.

An overhanging branch from a tree slammed with such force against their window, cracking the glass. Max was startled awake. Sitting up in bed, he looked at the damage. Through it he could see the branch repeatedly slamming against the window. Looking over at the other bed, he saw that Cynthia was sound asleep. Helpless and fearing the worst, he cowered against the pillow and hugged the bedclothes. For a brief moment he felt safe. Then, through the broken glass, illuminated by a bright flash of lightning, he saw it. An evanescent form with soulless eyes.

CHAPTER EIGHT

Paralyzed by fear and unable to scream, Max feeling helpless, shrank back in his bed, to hide beneath the covers. His mouth was dry and his entire body trembled, preventing him from moving. Suddenly, he desperately needed to use the bathroom. Daring himself to quickly look back at the window, he realized that the horrifying figure had vanished. Despite mustering up all his strength he hesitated to leave the safety of the room, fearing that the entity would reappear elsewhere in the house and this time cause him harm. He was certain by the scary and shimmering appearance, that he had seen a ghost. Max decided to remain under the bedclothes, be as still as possible, hoping not to be detected in the event that the sinister form returned. As he waited for morning, his bladder gave way. Now Max had another emotion other than fear to deal with. Embarrassment.

The storm had subsided by the time dawn broke. Max decided to clean himself up and get rid of the damp sheets before the housekeeper found them. Quietly he made his way down the hall, but before reaching the stairs, Tim emerged from his room.

"Where do you think you're going?" the older boy demanded to know, blocking the stairwell.

"I'm going to get some breakfast," Max lied.

"Really? Carrying your sheets?" Tim said, grabbing at the bundle in Max's arms. "Eeww!" He exclaimed, pulling back his hand wiping the urine residue on Max's pajama top. Max began to cry, drawing attention from his father, who had heard the exchange of words.

"What is going on here?" Max Senior asked, looking at both boys.

"He peed his pants. Little Maxwell is a bed wetter," Tim mocked.

"Alright, that's enough Tim."

"I saw a ghost in the window during the storm," Max tried to explain, hoping that his cousin would leave him alone and his father be of comfort.

"There's no such thing as ghosts. It's all nonsense," his father stated, making it clear that he did not wish to discuss the matter further. To young Max's dismay, his mother, a loving woman devoted to her children, was of the same opinion as her husband. Nobody believed him.

CHAPTER NINE

The memory of that night was vivid and now cemented in Max's conscious mind. Max analyzed more closely the enormous and damaging impact it could have had on his own emotional development, had it thankfully not been suppressed by the brain's natural psychological defense mechanisms.

He thought back to Olivia and her constant state of hypervigilance during their sessions. It dawned on him that had she disclosed the *multiple* events, it would have been easy to give a diagnosis of Early Onset Childhood Psychosis. A diagnosis of this severity would have meant the need for pharmacological treatment that came with an array of side effects. The stigma of mental illness would have changed her life forever. Max concluded that she *had* been smart. This diary had been her chance to confide in him without prejudice or fear of the consequences. But why now? She was dead. Untouchable.

Max felt emotionally weighed down by his own revived traumatic memory and a mixture of belated sorrow and sympathy for the once young Olivia. He closed the album and sat quietly for a moment, honoring his feelings, before returning it to the shelf. Leaning against the book shelf, he closed his eyes and steadied his breathing. The library was eerily quiet.

Unexpectedly, Max had the impression of being watched. Slowly opening his eyes he looked around the room but saw nothing. The air felt different against his skin, as if charged with an invisible veil of electricity. Then he heard something. Straining to listen he held his breath. Nothing. Apprehensive, Max decided to return to reading Olivia's diary in the safety and warmth of the sun. Moving towards the door leading out to the veranda, he walked through what felt like a cold spot. Just air from the air conditioning vent, he rationalized. Wasn't it?

CHAPTER TEN

I must have been nine when I had another visitation. I had woken up that morning with a lingering pain in my lower abdomen. My mother took my temperature and made me a warm chamomile tea, which I regurgitated. Worried, she called our family doctor who, after examining me, arranged for an urgent admission to hospital.

Diagnosis: Acute Abdomen, which later I found out was appendicitis. Most think that one is safe in a hospital, but for those who see more, it's a hive of activity. I was lying in bed on the paediatric ward recovering from the simple operation. I had the room to myself, as the patient next to me had been discharged earlier that morning. My family had come to visit that afternoon, with Carl sneaking in jelly beans to give me strength and something to look forward to—hospital food was not the greatest.

Shortly after they had left, a man walked into my room unannounced. At first I thought it was another doctor coming to check on me. He was a stocky man wearing a white coat with a stethoscope around his neck. I smiled nervously but unlike my other doctors he didn't smile back, something I found unusual. In fact, he was silent. His face was gaunt, its features unclear and mildly distorted. As he neared the bed his feet made an odd sound. I looked over the edge of my bed and to my horror discovered that he had no legs. Confused and frightened I asked myself how this could be.

He floated closer. I shrank back into the pillows, pulling the sheets up around me and shutting my eyes as tightly as I could, willing him to disappear. When I finally decided to take a peek, he was levitating so close to me, with his stethoscope in his hands and an eerie facial expression, giving me the unmistakable impression that I was about to be strangled! Without hesitation and ignoring the discomfort from the incision in my right lower flank, I bolted out of bed, out of the room and toward the stairwell. With all my strength I managed to push open the metal door and race down several flights of stairs.

I am not entirely sure how, but I found myself in the basement. Looking for another way out, still frantic, I became disorientated and lost in the vast underground corridors. Then, I saw a sign: 'MORGUE'. My senses were now in overdrive, such that I could hear and sense the legless man close distance between us. Alarmed, I entered the morgue to hide.

There were two tables, one of which supported a lifeless body. Hiding behind the second slab, I held my breath and listened out for my persecutor. I could hear my heart beat throbbing in my ears. The wound in my side burned. Looking down at it I could see blood weeping though the bandage. I placed one hand over it to stop the bleeding. The air was cool. My breathing was shallow in part due to my fragile physical state, but I also did not want my warm breath to be a visible contrast in the cooler environment, giving me away.

The door to the morgue opened and slammed shut. I sat quietly, listening. Footsteps drew closer, then stopped. The silence of the place was deafening. I couldn't help it but I started to whimper. I held my hand in front of my mouth to stop the sound from escaping my lips. The footsteps started again, this time toward me. I closed my eyes keeping them shut as tight as possible, forcing myself not to look at him.

"Hey sweetie," a friendly female voice said. Looking up I saw a young lady dressed in scrubs kneeling in front of me. "What are you doing here?" she enquired, extending her hand. I took it and felt instant comfort. She was real, made of flesh and bone.

"I was looking for the bathroom and got lost," I lied, something I'd become accustomed to doing.

"Come on, honey, let me take you back to your room. What's your name?" she asked.

"Olivia Croft," I replied, now less frightened.

The lady introduced herself as Dr. Samantha White before placing a call to the hospital switchboard, to establish which of the three paediatric wards I belonged to. As we walked back to the surgical section, we came across a gallery of framed photos of both medical and nursing staff, who had once worked at the hospital. I stopped in front of a portrait. It was him!

"Who is that?" I asked Sam, my savior. She studied the man in the picture with a nostalgic expression before answering, "That was my father, Professor David H. White".

"Oh," I remarked, wondering how such a nice lady could have a scary parent.

"He made a big mistake during one of his operations. The patient didn't make it. He felt a lot of shame and guilt. He decided to leave his profession and everyone behind."

I knew exactly what she meant, but wasn't going to add to her anguish by telling her about his visit.

One day maybe, but not today. I learned something valuable from this dark encounter, namely that tragedy can strike anyone, leaving a painful impression not just in a loved one's heart, but also on earth.

****

Max rested the diary on his chest for a brief moment before deciding to read on. Glancing at his watch, he calculated that there was still time for another chapter before his routine late morning coffee. Just as he turned to the next page, his mobile vibrated in his pocket. Retrieving it, he stared at the screen and chose to ignore the caller.

CHAPTER ELEVEN

After nearly a week in hospital, my parents were able to take me home. It was a relief to all that I was on the mend, but still being weak, the doctor ordered me to rest.

My dreams were becoming more bizarre and disjointed. The visitations had begun to haunt me in my sleep, leaving me tired and edgy during the day.

One dream I recall well was that of a young woman standing outside a house, pointing to its roof. Her nightgown was riddled with what look like blooded cuts. Now I can recognize and label them as stab wounds. I knew that she had died and her spirit was still lingering, for some reason showing itself to me. I wonder whether she appeared in my dream rather than as a form in my room to avoid frightening me.

That morning, I overheard my father, over breakfast, discussing a criminal case with my grandfather (at the time a retired judge). Both had been unaware that I could hear them as I approached the kitchen.

"They can't find the murder weapon," my father said. "This poor girl gets stabbed and I'm supposed to convict without any real evidence?" he continued, exasperated.

"Well, at least you have a body. In some cases there isn't even that," Grandfather commented.

"They've looked everywhere. Nothing. Ziltch!"

"Have the detectives checked the rooftop or the gutters?" I asked, coming forward.

Both starred at me for a moment then looked at each other, before my father asked, "How long have you been standing there?"

"Long enough to hear the part about the missing weapon," I volunteered.

"Well," my grandfather began. "My little Nancy Drew, where do you think it could be?" He asked with amusement and affection.

"Have they checked the rooftop or gutters?" I repeated.

"No, why?" he asked.

"Most people focus on hiding things in the ground, so that's where they search. Nobody thinks to look up where something may have been tossed, perhaps in a hurry," I explained.

"She has a point," Dad said finally, reaching for the phone presumably to call someone in charge of the search. He didn't need to ask me to leave the breakfast room. I did so of my own accord as my job to deliver the message had been done. The following night the same woman reappeared, but this time, in my room. She was smiling.

CHAPTER TWELVE

Sean had returned from his game of golf and other social engagements, and was taking a shower when the phone rang. Max was getting ready to attend dinner at Harvey's. While slipping on a shirt he answered.

"Hi, honey!" a chipper voice greeted him. It was Pam, his wife.

"Hey stranger, long time no speak," he replied teasingly.

"Oh, it's only effectively been five days," she replied, knowing that he missed her as much as she did him.

"Sean and I are having dinner with Harvey and Shirley this evening. How are things in Chile? Is it expensive?" he asked, always concerned about how far his dollar would stretch.

"Don't worry, it's quite cheap here and we got a great deal for the hotel," she reassured.

After exchanging a few more pleasantries, Sean joined the conversation in the background. It was a typical manner of the Stein family to have a three-way conversation when one of them was overseas.

The call ended with all three blowing kisses at each other through the receiver. Max didn't feel the need to tell Pam about the diary when she enquired about how he was passing the time. Olivia would have wanted only *him* to know the truth. Even in death he would respect confidentiality.

The evening with Harvey and Shirley was pleasant. Once again their host pulled out the 'famous' board for a game of Scrabble.

"I knew this would happen," Sean stated, amused at his father's enthusiasm for the word game.

The game proceeded with a lot of banter and laughter between the foursome.

"Seven letter word starting with a V, third letter S and last one an E," Sean said pensively at one of his turns.

"It's worth a lot of points," Harvey commented, winking at him.

As the group patiently waited for Sean to find a word, Max became aware of a faint whisper surrounding his head. Intrigued, he strained to hear it more clearly, as it slowly grew louder.

"Vestige! **V-E-S-T-I-G-E**," Max impulsively announced, startling his friends. Was it coincidence that this particular word had come up in the game? And who or what had whispered into his ears? Max didn't know what to make of it. All he knew was that he had been reading the diary of a spirit he had encountered in his office a couple of days prior, filled with paranormal accounts. Slightly apprehensive about the obscure hint 'given' to him and remorseful for embarrassing Sean, he fell silent.

"It means the remnants of something that once existed," Sean informed them reading from an old Oxford dictionary. Max continued to say nothing. For the first time ever, he wanted the game to end. He felt consumed by the urge to get home. Back to Olivia.

CHAPTER THIRTEEN

In the summer of 1992, my father took us to Italy. It was our first overseas trip as a family. We toured Rome, Florence, Siena, taking in all the wonderful sights and learning about the history. The last city on our itinerary was Venice. I, and even more so my mother, greatly anticipated the experience of floating along the canals in a Gondola.

"How romantic," she said, leaning on my father's shoulder as we boarded the water taxi that would take us from the Marco Polo airport to our hotel. My father was always keen to read up about a place he was visiting, including the accommodation he had booked. His eternal hunger for ongoing knowledge was something that I admired. I think his interest concerning the mysterious uncertainty of life and tenacity to find facts to support the truth made him a good lawyer. These characteristics shaped my own academic journey, propelling me to follow the same career path.

"This particular hotel has a grand entrance decorated in a baroque style. It was once owned by a rich merchant who had married into nobility, but did not live long enough to enjoy his wealth," he read to us from the travel guide as we rode the taxi.

"Oh? What happened?" Carl asked, keen to learn more.

"Nothing much, it doesn't say," he replied, abruptly closing the book. My brother and I looked at one another, wondering what could have happened. I already had my own hypothesis but wasn't going to share it, already dreading what I may encounter.

We got to the hotel, which looked imposing in its structure and décor, coupled with a sinister atmosphere. The staff were friendly and very welcoming, almost too eager to please which made the place seem even more creepy.

"Maybe there's a dead body hidden in the walls," Carl whispered to me as we were escorted to our suite. I didn't reply. You can imagine why not, can't you Dr. Stein?

****

Shocked, Max stopped reading. He looked away from the diary and focused on repeating a verse of his favorite song, a learned strategy to calm himself. He had not expected this. It was a subtle but powerful message directed at him! Still shaken, he poured himself a Cognac, gulping it down before pouring a second and drinking it less hastily. Slowly the alcohol soothed his nerves enabling the seasoned psychologist to read on.

****

One night, while fast asleep in a bed that was far too large for my small frame, I was awakened by the sobbing sounds of a woman. At first I thought that I was dreaming, but soon became aware that the sound was real. Sitting up in bed, I listened, wondering if anyone else could hear the cries of deep sorrow. The sound became more desperate, so I decided to investigate.

I dangled my legs over the edge of the bed before slowly and carefully sliding off onto the cold wooden floor. I tiptoed to the door, opened it and hesitantly peered into the hallway. The sound grew louder, its origin on my left. With trepidation I stepped into the large, chilly hall, which was sparsely furnished. A small bistro setting consisting of a table and two chairs created shadows that loomed over the far side of the area. The growing chill in the air fueled my fear, causing me to regret the decision I had made. Just as I was about to retreat back to the safety of my room, I saw her. A dark unearthly form sitting on one of the chairs, her head bowed and hands covering her face. Her cries pierced my soul.

I was overwhelmed with a sense of grief which I did not yet comprehend. Then, abruptly, the crying stopped. Was she aware of being watched? I stood perfectly still, holding my breath. The figure slowly turned its head and looked in my direction. I was still not sure if she had seen me. My heart pounded so loudly that I feared my eardrums would rupture. Gradually before my eyes, the bereaved spirit faded until it disappeared completely. I stood for a moment contemplating my next move, as the sadness in the air lingered. I decided to return to the safety of my bed and wait until morning when everything would seem 'normal' again.

I never found out what tragedy had taken place at the old hotel and was relieved at the end of our family holiday to return home. Another thing I learned over time, was that while idea of home being a sanctuary was comforting, there was no place to hide from the spirit world. They were everywhere.

CHAPTER FOURTEEN

The forecast of a classic seasonal storm had been broadcast on the evening news, leading Max to secure all windows and place the outdoor furniture in the small garden shed. He then went to bed, and within minutes of his head resting on the soft feather pillow, he was asleep.

Outside the storm front slowly approached the coastline. Thunder clouds built to great heights, becoming saturated with moisture, ready to unleash large drops of rain destined to drench anything they touched. The wind strengthened to a crescendo, howling though the trees and rattling the old wooden window shutters. Max awoke to the sound of thunder. He lay still waiting for the deafening noise to subside. Then more lightning lit his bedroom, revealing something unimaginable. Sitting up in bed he called out gently, "Sean?"

His son was kneeling in the middle of the room. A faint sound of sobbing surrounding him. Sean then stood and moved through the closed door and out of sight. Panicked, Max jumped out of bed, and without putting on his slippers, swung open his bedroom door and hurried down the hall towards his boy's room. More lightning, then, another crack of thunder reverberated throughout the house. Reaching his son's room, with a sweaty hand, he grabbed the handle to yank the door open. Sean looked peaceful and was sound asleep.

His heart racing, beads of sweat building on his brow, a taste of bile filling his mouth, Max was unsure of what he had just witnessed. Was it a warning from beyond? One thing was certain. This was no dream.

****

The next morning, Sean energetically bounced into the kitchen and poured himself a glass of orange juice. He was wearing the latest fashion in sports gear he'd purchased just before the holidays. Max, leaning against the counter, arms folded, watched as he finished the juice then helped himself to a bowl of cereal.

"Hey, hey, hey! Today is the day!" Sean announced enthusiastically. The day for the much anticipated skydiving adventure had finally arrived.

"We're not going," Max replied. Sean looked up from his breakfast and paused. A look of surprise and disappointment crossed his face.

"Dad, why not? We had this planned for, like, ages," he protested confused.

"It's too dangerous," Max said, pouring a cup of coffee.

"So is crossing the street in New York!" the youth retorted.

"We're not going! Period!" Max stated firmly, his tone growing angry. He picked up his coffee and walked out onto the porch, leaving his son to deal with the decision.

Sean was dumbfounded. He couldn't understand his father's sudden change of heart and hostility toward him.

He decided to keep to himself, not wanting to aggrieve him any further. Sean was worried about him. For now, he would just observe, but he wondered if the behavior had anything to do with that diary he had been reading non-stop. Peeking through the window, he saw Max standing in the garden, smiling while staring off into the distance.

CHAPTER FIFTEEN

After the experience in Venice, I found myself withdrawing from the social and recreational activities I had once enjoyed. I was frightened by not knowing what to expect from the other dimension and about how long I could keep up the pretense that all was well. The disrupted sleep pattern, constant lethargy and difficulty concentrating on my school work were becoming obvious. The teachers decided to meet with the principal to discuss their concern about my declining academic performance, who in turn called in my parents.

"Mrs. Croft," the principal began, "Olivia seems distracted and if I may say so, troubled".

"Yes. We have noticed some changes, but will look into it," my mother assured him.

If they had only known the truth. I wasn't just 'troubled' like most kids at some stage in their development, but haunted!

My parents' concern escalated when one day I refused to attend my own birthday party. All my friends were waiting in the garden, but despite my mother's best efforts, I wouldn't join them. I hadn't slept all night, having been kept awake by incessant whispering in my room. To drown out the unearthly echoing sounds, I listened to music through my headphones. My father, to save face, provided our guests with a plausible explanation. He simply stated that I was feeling unwell. It was the truth.

Carl took over the festivities. I gathered from the joyous laughter in the garden outside my window, that he was doing a good job at keeping everyone entertained. I could always count on him to be supportive and protective, but he couldn't protect me from everything.

My parents consulted a specialist recommended by our family doctor, an expert for children with emotional problems. They made an appointment, hoping he would provide answers explaining my steadily increasing withdrawal from others and disinterest in food, which had resulted in significant weight loss. I could not bring myself to be honest with my family and tell them that the stress I was under was related to various encounters with specters. I still couldn't quite understand why I was being followed and at times tormented by them. I felt very alone.

The day came when I first met Dr. Fritz. He was an older gentleman with short white hair and light blue eyes, who spoke quickly but didn't mince his words. After an hour's consultation with my parents, it was my turn to speak with him on my own.

"Your parents have told me many good things about you, but are worried that things have changed," he began with a slight foreign accent. I nodded. "So, can you tell me what is bothering you? I am here to help, so do not be afraid," he reassured, hoping I would be more forthcoming.

I just sat and stared at him. There was nothing I wanted to say, for I knew that he could not help me. Half an hour elapsed with this Dr. Fritz asking me to draw a picture of my family and talk about anything that came into my mind.

I didn't engage. It was as if I had shut out the entire world, keeping my fears hidden.

He finally summoned my parents, telling them that he wanted to admit me to his unit—which turned out to be a psychiatric ward—for a period of observation.

"What's wrong with her?" my parents asked.

"I am not sure but there may be an element of hysteria or even emerging psychosis."

"Hysteria?" they said in unison. "What did she tell you?" they demanded to know, growing more concerned.

"Nothing. Which is why I think it's important to observe and find out," the specialist suggested.

My parents agreed to a voluntary admission for a maximum of forty-eight hours observation, after which they would be insisting on taking me home. So, with the necessary paperwork completed, I had my first, and thankfully last, introduction to the children's psychiatric ward.

CHAPTER SIXTEEN

I don't know what my parents were thinking in agreeing to have me admitted to this unit for disturbed kids. In truth, the other children weren't aggressive but, like me, had problems. I briefly made friends with an older girl by the name of Gwen. We talked about school, family and being in the unit, as I watched her pedantically rearrange all the information pamphlets so that they stood neatly in their plastic containers. She explained her diagnosis to me as Obsessive Compulsive Disorder, or in short, OCD. Her company made my stay less traumatic, however, I had already made a promise to myself that I would not stay longer than the forty-eight hours. My strategy was not to display withdrawn behavior and interact appropriately with others, especially the staff, so they could be reassured that I was not a danger to anyone or psychotic.

Dr. Fritz came to see me with another junior doctor. The senior clinician led the interview, leaving his junior colleague to make a handful of enquiries. This time I answered all their questions, conscious not to give up my secret. They eventually got the picture of a ten year old who was suffering from social anxiety, thanks to my carefully crafted answers. This was a more acceptable diagnosis, certainly to me and to them, far removed from the initial impression of hysteria or possible psychosis. The upside was that social anxiety was usually treated in an outpatient setting. Hurray!

My parents were relieved that their daughter hadn't gone crazy, so to celebrate they took me and Carl out for dinner. It was while waiting for our meals to arrive that Dad divulged to us a shameful part of his family background. A part nobody wanted to ever discuss. His grandmother and one of his uncles had suffered from mental illness. We didn't dare ask questions, despite the awkward silence that followed the revelation. Knowing what I knew about myself, it left me wondering if they, too, had possibly been misunderstood and consequently misdiagnosed.

****

Those last words, 'misunderstood and misdiagnosed', struck another nerve with Max, as had the earlier entry about not being believed. Max paused for a moment. Then, after taking a deep breath, read on.

CHAPTER SEVENTEEN

My first session with Dr. Maxwell Stein was anything but frightening. He had been carefully sought out by our family doctor and was considered an expert in childhood anxiety disorders. He was youthful in appearance, always clean shaven, wearing his shoulder length brown curly hair in a ponytail. Behind thin rimmed spectacles were a pair of hazel eyes, exuding empathy.

His demeanor was calming and manner pleasant. We sat on the floor opposite each other.

"Couches are for adults. I prefer sitting on the floor on a cushion," he began, explaining his less conventional modus operandi.

"Ok" I answered.

"Olivia, are you comfortable or would you prefer a bean bag?" He asked, implying that I was a young person with choices. So different from Dr.Fritz.

"I am fine," I replied, feeling more relaxed and hoping just maybe I could provide him with a bit of insight into my inner world. In truth, I was desperate to tell someone. I was tired of feeling burdened and emotionally isolated.

"What do you like doing for fun?"

"Lots of things, I guess," I replied, not sure where he was going with his question.

"Do you like word games, such as Scrabble?"

"Do you like Scrabble, Doctor Stein?" I asked, wondering how he would react with a patient asking questions.

"I do. I have it here," he said smiling warmly. "Shall we have a quick game?"

Not wanting to disappoint and curious by his different approach, I agreed.

Reflecting back, his was a smart way to develop a therapeutic alliance, assess intelligence and use the game as a form of word association to draw out what lay beneath the conscious mind.

We played. I am certain that subconsciously I dropped a few clues for him to work out on his own. I hoped that maybe in time, with a little bit of my help, Dr. Stein would put together all the pieces of the puzzle and revise my diagnosis to: Haunted.

****

Max closed the diary and placed it to one side. He remembered that first session very well. The young Olivia masked her fear almost to perfection. Now, he recalled she had spelled the words 'ghost' and 'spook' out on the game's board. Had it been a coincidence or intentional? Intrigued, Max decided that there was still time before Sean got back from visiting his best friend to read just a little more.

CHAPTER EIGHTEEN

As the sessions with Dr. Stein continued, I began feeling that he was doing his best to uncover the trigger for my anxious nature. Let's face it, anyone who had regular contact with ghosts would be left uncertain about their journey in life and at times rather intimidated by even benign events. Doc, as I now called him, had gone as far as to give me a diagnosis of an anxiety disorder, but remained optimistic that in time it would resolve. My parents were very grateful. I, on the other hand, was not so optimistic.

One afternoon, as always, I arrived punctually to one of my sessions to find a German Shepherd laying at Doc's feet. The animal lifted its head to look at me before standing and slowly moving in my direction. For the first time, Doc seemed sad, but was trying to mask his emotions with frequent smiling. The large dog walked around me, sniffing my clothing. I could feel a gentle tickle on my skin just as I had experienced as an infant during my first visitation. I was tempted to reach out and pat him, but knew better. Then the dog returned to sit by his master letting out a grunt.

"You seem sad today, Doc," I observed.

"You are very perceptive," he said, smiling. "Our dog passed away last night. Old age, the vet explained."

"I'm sorry to hear," I began, before he interrupted me by saying, *"The strange thing is that I can still feel him around me. I can even smell him."*

"He's probably in doggie heaven," I volunteered gently, aware that its spirit was in the same room with us. Doc smiled. In truth I had no idea what animal ghosts were capable of, which unsettled me.

The silence between the gaps in our conversation was deafening. Suddenly, there was a loud vocalization (of the canine variety), causing both of us to jump to our feet.

"You heard that, didn't you?" he asked, now almost joyous. I nodded while keeping a close watch on the dog, which was now standing and moving toward the window. We both stood perfectly still. As it leaped through the closed window, a vase was knocked to the floor by its tail. I remained calm. Dr. Stein excused himself and terminated our session earlier than usual. He needed to grieve.

****

Reading those last words, Max felt completely overcome by a whirlwind of emotions. Tears ran down his cheeks, dropping onto and moistening his dark cotton shirt. Quietly, Max cried. He wasn't sure whether he was grieving for a lost opportunity as a clinician to understand better or for something else.

CHAPTER NINETEEN

Years have passed since I last saw Dr. Maxwell Stein in a therapeutic context. Despite not revealing my experiences and allowing him to understand me fully, I did learn techniques on how to relax. These came in handy. The ghostly encounters continued, contrary to what I had read in books describing the paranormal, where it was suggested that as children grew older, they were less open to perceiving the spirit world.

I could see, hear, smell and feel them. It was difficult to ignore them while walking down the street trying to go about my daily business. They would follow me and try to interact with me. One entity, an elderly male, would recite poetry.

In truth, not all were frightening, some rather comforting. I fondly recall during my years at Harvard Law regular encounters with the spirit of an old judge. Dressed in his black cloak, and always carrying a briefcase, he would accompany me into the hall where I would sit for my exams. He always stood in the same corner as if waiting for the examination to officially commence. Then without fail, his image would slowly fade, before disappearing completely. Sometimes, I would see his essence drift across the campus grounds where students, hurrying to lectures would walk straight through him. More than once I spied him vanishing into the trunk of a large oak tree. Although I saw him on several occasions, he never once spoke or uttered a sound. Unlike some other specters, he had a quiet and calming presence that I appreciated and respected.

There was something vaguely familiar about the judge. Looking through the archives of the city's lawyers and judges I had hoped to learn more about him, but it was not meant to be. So the mysterious judge continued to roam the university grounds incognito. Even though I never learned his name, I believed that he was there in some way to provide moral support in times of stress.

****

A nostalgic feeling descended upon Max. The idea of a ghost being of comfort to the living would have been considered preposterous by many of his colleagues. Yet, Olivia's revelation of the phantom judge reminded him of his sister Cynthia. Her death had been sudden and unexpected. The autopsy performed at her husband's request had been inconclusive. In life Cynthia had been his rock, especially after the violent murder of his high school sweetheart by a convicted murderer who was out on parole.

Max retrieved the photo of Cynthia he kept in his wallet and held it gently, smiling down at the image. Even now, she was still a comfort to him during difficult times. Max was starting to realize that in fact not only was he learning a lot about Olivia, but also through her accounts, about himself. The diary had dredged up the past.

Was this a good thing?

The piercing ringtone of the landline echoed through the silence in the cottage, interrupting his train of thought.

Getting up from where he had been sitting comfortably and irritated by the intrusion, Max walked into the foyer to answer it. It was Sean.

"Hey, Dad," he began casually. "Is it ok if I bring a couple of friends over for dinner tonight?"

"Sure," his father replied, feigning enthusiasm, wondering who would join them and what he would prepare for the impromptu evening meal. So many of Sean's friends were fussy eaters. Tonight Max was in no mood to play host. He just wanted to get back to the diary. *His* diary. After replacing the receiver in its cradle, he returned to the comfort of the sofa and Olivia's words.

CHAPTER TWENTY

As mentioned earlier, some encounters were troublesome. Like this next one.

My brother Carl dreamed of being an airline pilot, so he studied aviation at college. We both shared an interest in flying. Fascinated by aerobatic displays, every year without fail, we'd attend the annual American Aero show.

Carl convinced me to get my private pilot license, as it would give me the freedom to travel independently around our vast country while enjoying my passion. I enrolled in a small flying school and began taking lessons. The training was awesome, made exciting by my very experienced instructor, Mitchell. Carl, myself and Mitch, as I'd call him, celebrated when I finally got my wings. It took a little longer than expected due to my other commitments as a law student.

Not long after, it all changed when I had my worst ghostly encounter. I was preparing to do a cross country flight with Mitch as part of a scheduled flight review. This was procedure for all pilots to ensure that aviation standards were being maintained.

"Hey, Olivia!" Mitch said, walking up to me with his pilot bag and clipboard in hand. "All set to go?"

"Yep. I've logged the flight plan and just finished pre-flight on the aircraft."

"Any glitches?" he asked as we walked from the main building to the hangars.

"None," I said smiling, excited to get airborne as soon as possible.

It was a beautiful day, not a cloud in the sky and no rain forecast. The winds were light, coming from the east and due to remain such for the duration of our two-hour flight. Perfect!

Once in the cockpit, I donned my headset and ran methodically through the checklists. Mitch sat quietly, allowing me to focus. I taxied the four seater Cessna to the holding point and waited for the tower to give me clearance for our take-off. Smoothly advancing the throttle until full power was reached, the aircraft overcame its initial inertia and accelerated down the runway. Once the 'rotate' speed had been established, I gently pulled back the control column, lifting the nose slightly and easing the aircraft into the air. As the distance between the undercarriage and ground grew and with nothing but a clear blue sky ahead of us, I had a feeling of quiet euphoria.

Everything was going according to plan until an hour into the flight. I chose a cruise altitude of 5,500 feet to get best range while still preserving fuel. The ambient temperature at that altitude stayed pleasant on a warm day such as this one. However, feeling cold Mitch reached for his sweater. The temperature gage indicated 23 degrees Celsius, but it felt much cooler. I too, was now aware of the shift in temperature. Glancing at the gage again, I noted that the figure had dropped by four degrees. I pressed on, trying to ignore what I dreaded. Mitch opened the vent to allow warm air from the heat exchanger into the cabin, but it made no difference.

Suddenly, I felt a chilling presence behind me in the back seat. The hair on the back of my neck stood erect like soldiers. As part of training you learn early on, that flying the aircraft and maintain control of it, is paramount to dealing with any threat within or outside of the cockpit. 'Fly the plane,' I repeated to myself as part of my internal dialogue. During the course of my training, it had been a mantra to me.

Keeping my composure, I refused to look at what sat behind me. Then, I felt the cold dense mass of air press up against my back, as if it was attempting to penetrate my body. Through my peripheral vision, I saw a wasted, red-raw, burned hand extend between myself and Mitch, reaching for the throttle. Alarmed, I watched as the throttle slowly moved to a lower setting. The sound of the engine changed from a hum to a deeper tone and the nose of the aircraft pitched down. Mitch glanced over at me. I smiled slightly nervously. To avoid losing altitude I gently advanced it again until the power setting for a cruise had been restored.

Then it happened again. We both could see it now. My hand was nowhere near the lever.

"What's going on?" Mitch asked, alarmed as I returned it to the desired setting.

I couldn't bring myself to tell him. I knew we had a 'passenger'. Quickly, I glanced behind me only to see an empty back seat. Maybe it was over.

We flew for a few more minutes and I had started to relax, but then the hand reappeared, closed the throttle completely and held it firmly in that position, starving the engine of fuel and power. Instinctively I set the aircraft up for its glide speed while Mitch battled with the throttle. It was serious. We were going to have to land somewhere. Aware *of the wind's direction from the latest forecast, choosing a field in which to land was my priority. Mitch, panicked and confused, was expressing his discomfort with a few choice words.*

"MAYDAY, MAYDAY, MAYDAY!" I called through the radio after setting our transponder on the emergency code 7700. The air traffic controller had heard me and responded. For a split moment I was undecided what to state as our emergency. I cautiously chose "engine failure" and, as per protocol, provided other relevant information. Then, there was nothing. Silence. The radio and the electrical system died.

I glanced at Mitch, who was no longer holding on to the throttle, but just sitting, sweaty and pale, his stare vacant. I knew that I would have to conduct a landing without the use of flaps, since their operation required electricity. Fortunately there was a large field without much cattle, in which I managed to land safely. A wave of relief was overshadowed by the realization that Mitch was dead.

The expression 'stress can kill' is very true and also applies to fear. This had been too much for me. I never flew again.

****

Max sat in shock, his entire body quivering and heart racing. The intensity of this story was overwhelming, making him feel as if he had been in that airplane with Mitch and Olivia, experiencing the dread and impending doom. Never could he have imagined something like this happening to anyone. He swallowed hard. Before doing anything else, he reached for the bottle of Scotch. He desperately needed a drink.

CHAPTER TWENTY-ONE

In spring break of the last year of my law studies, I attended a party, full of hope and gleefully anticipating graduation at the end of the year. I had worked hard and was ready to let my hair down for once.

My friends were young, intelligent people who knew how to have a good time. Being studious, my track record for partying was poor, so they saw this as an opportunity to make sure that I lived up to the occasion. There was drinking, dancing and other activities I'd rather not discuss.

"You've got to just chill out and hang out," Tom said as we approached the frat house.

"Yeah, you are too serious, girl. Time to let your hair down," Kate agreed. Our friend Gemma, who was already there, came to greet us at the door and introduced us to some of her friends. This was really not my scene. I wanted to turn on my heels and head home. However, not wanting to offend anybody, I stayed and tried to blend in. A drunk guy, whom I might confess was rather cute, asked me to dance.

"Hey, what's your name?" he asked leading me to the dance floor.

"Olivia," I replied.

"Well, you are one lucky girl, Olivia. I have a great—"

Before he could finish the sentence, another girl slid her way between us, allowing me to disengage from his sweaty grip. What a relief!

At one point during the evening, my three close friends, other two acquaintances and I, left the rowdy crowd and went up into the attic of the house. Gemma pulled out a Ouija board. The hairs on my arms stood on end, my hands started shaking as I suddenly became aware of a presence in the small dusty space. In the far corner of the attic, a sliver of what seemed like mist hovered. I wanted out of there.

"Guys, I don't think we should play with that thing," I said, hoping that they would agree. Regretfully, they just laughed and proceeded to set the mysterious looking board onto a small table.

"Come on 'livia. What, are you scared?" Tom teased. Torn between staying and wanting to flee, I decided against my better judgment to stay. Kate lit several candles, creating an even more dark and sinister atmosphere. The session began innocently enough, with attempts to be serious broken with giggles. Tom placed a bible on the board, playing out the role of exorcist.

Then the mood quickly turned violent. Out of nowhere a chair flew at Tom, missing his head by inches before smashing against the wall. I understood the spirit had felt taunted. Tom, the usual prankster of the group, was trembling and pale with a look of horror in his eyes. He broke away from the circle of conjuring, slid like a navy seal down the attic's trapdoor stairs and, screaming for his life, ran into the dark night. I followed, feeling compelled to help.

"Tom! Stop!" I called after him. He kept running. I gave chase. He reached a main road, his body swerving through its traffic in an attempt to cross it. I couldn't follow. Someone was holding me firmly by the arms. I looked around but saw nobody. Still almost concreted onto the spot, I helplessly watched a small truck career into Tom, sending his body airborne to land in a heap on the other side of the road.

Cars screeched to a halt. The smell of burned tire rubber filled the air. Whatever had been holding me now released its grip, but still in shock, I couldn't move.

My friends finally caught up with me just as the ambulance arrived.

"What happened?" Gemma asked.

Angry and upset, I didn't reply. To anyone at the site it would have been obvious as to what had just occurred. Tom was pronounced dead at the scene by one of the paramedics, who used his fingers to gently close his eyes, and then covered the body.

A gentle flow of cool air touched the back of my neck. I turned and saw him. A young man, I'm guessing not much older than seventeen. In spite of having a sad expression, he gave me a weak smile. I reached out, trying to touch his face. There was nothing, for he had vanished.

Tom's funeral was attended by over a hundred mourners. Standing a few feet away from the crowd I spotted the young man again. He beckoned me to follow him. Grateful for saving me that terrible night, I did. He stopped in front of a grave. The tombstone read: Ross H. Willis. Then once again his form faded before vanishing. I later found out through newspaper archives that he had died tragically on that same *road, on the same date, two years prior. Like Tom's, another young life just wasted.*

I never spoke of that night to Gemma or any of the others. In fact, I cut all ties with them. I was angry, believing this could have been prevented had they listened and taken my warning seriously. Perhaps I should have tried harder to talk them out of it, knowing what I do. My anger was soon replaced by guilt.

CHAPTER TWENTY-TWO

Without warning, the front door to the cottage swung open.

"Dad! We're here!" Sean announced, inviting his best friend George and the new girlfriend into the living room.

"Hey there, son," Max greeted, setting down his reading material and trying to appear relaxed.

"What's for dinner?" George asked. Max had known him for years, and was like an uncle to him.

"*Penne al Pomodoro,*" he replied, before continuing, "That's pasta with tomato sauce, of course accompanied by a healthy garden salad."

The group gathered around the kitchen counter, all volunteering to participate in preparing the evening meal.

The phone rang just as they were about to sit down to dinner. Max answered hoping it would be his wife, and it was.

"How are things?" he asked, pausing to give her time to share all the lovely sites she'd visited and customs learned. Pamela was having a good time, which pleased him. Max returned to the table after a brief exchange of well wishes. Then, unexpectedly he was overcome by a sense of dread, but was unable to identify the reason for such an extreme shift in emotions. His son, noticing the change in his father's attitude over the last couple of days, and the solemn expression now clouding his face, grew more concerned. To lighten the conversation Sean chose to ask Sarah, George's new love interest, about herself.

"So, what made you venture into becoming a paramedic?" he asked her casually, pouring chilled water from a cooler into his glass.

"She's the best," George stated proudly.

"Well, I've always wanted to help people and like the diversity of each day on the job," she answered.

"Sarah was at the scene of that terrible jet ski accident only a few days ago. That poor woman losing her life," George started. "Thank goodness you now have a couple of days off to relax and not think about it, babe," he continued, blowing her a kiss.

"Wasn't she the daughter of one of our Supreme Court judges?" Sean asked.

"Yes, it was in all the newspapers. Croft I think was the name," George volunteered.

Max played with his food. He had lost his appetite. He wanted everyone to leave so that he could be alone. A dark cloak of sadness enveloped his soul. In order not embarrass his son, he drew on all his inner strength to remain composed until their guests left. It was such a relief to him when they finally did.

CHAPTER TWENTY-THREE

Sean cleared the dinner table and washed up. Max had poured himself a double Scotch on the rocks and watched his son from the door frame. He loved him dearly. The thought of anything happening to him was harrowing. He thought about the strange apparition of Sean in his room the night of the storm, still unable to make sense of it. Was it a warning of tragedy involving his son? Was Olivia trying to warn him through messages in her diary? The frightening alternative was that he was losing his grip on reality. Having worked in the field for many years, Max knew all too well that the early signs of insanity could be insidious.

"Thanks for having them here," Sean said sincerely, looking at his father for an indication that everything was ok. Max just nodded.

"I'm going to watch TV in my room. Want to join me?" he asked, nearing to where Max was standing.

"No, thanks," he replied, moving slightly so that Sean could walk past. Without attempting to make further conversation, both father and son kept to themselves by spending the rest of the night in separate quarters of the house.

Max downed his drink then poured another, consuming it quickly. He wondered whether it had been a coincidence that the same paramedic that had attended the accident site of 'his' Olivia, had just dined with them. 'Of all people in the Hamptons, that particular woman was here,' he pondered. Still ruminating, he reached for the bottle of Scotch and helped himself generously to a third drink.

In a state of growing anxiety, bordering on obsession, Max asked himself the same questions over and over again. What did it all mean? Was this some kind of a sign from beyond? Was Olivia warning him about Sean? The thoughts raced repetitively and his mind flashed on a constant visual loop back to that stormy night. It was getting too much for him to fathom.

Out of the corner of his eye, Max thought he saw the diary open of its own accord. He looked away, shut his eyes and counted to ten. 'Too much Scotch,' he thought.

Hesitantly he glanced back at where the book rested, willing it to be closed.

It was open.

CHAPTER TWENTY-FOUR

Sean lay on his futon bed watching a political documentary about the last Emperor of China. He loved history and social studies excelling in the subjects at school. His dream was to become a journalist, travel the world and eventually become a news anchor. He could hear his father climb the stairs and retire for the night. Disquieted by his father's moodiness and increased alcohol consumption, he contemplated whether to inform his mother and seek her advice. However, not wanting to worry her, he decided against it.

Feeling thirsty and unable to focus any further on the program, Sean turned the flat screen off and made his way down the stairs toward the kitchen. As he passed the living room, he paused. There on the coffee table he saw an almost empty bottle of Scotch and the diary. Curious about his father's preoccupation with it, he decided to sneak a quick look.

Approaching it, he noted that it was open. He hesitated for a moment, then, after looking over his shoulder to ensure he was alone, Sean picked it up and began reading.

"What the hell are you doing?" a voice barked at him from behind. Shocked, Sean spun around to find his father marching toward him.

"Nothing," he replied, trying to conceal the diary behind his back.

"Give me that!" Max bellowed, snatching it from him. "How dare you invade my privacy!"

Sean was horrified at the sudden change. It was uncharacteristic for either of his parents to behave in an aggressive manner. His father's expression was not just angry. It appeared as if something had 'possessed' him. His eyes seemed darker than normal and flickered from side to side, his jaw and fists were clenched shut, while the mysterious diary was firmly tucked away under his left armpit. Sean was speechless. For what seemed like an eternity, they stood in the moderately sized living room in silence. Until, at last, Max's body language returned to a more relaxed state.

"Oh! There it is," Max said, retrieving the diary from under his arm, as if completely unaware of what had just occurred. "Good night, son," he added and headed toward the stairs.

Sean stared after his father, not moving a muscle until he heard his father's bedroom door close upstairs.

CHAPTER TWENTY-FIVE

After graduation, my parents offered to send me on a well-deserved holiday. I chose Italy, still fascinated by the language, culture, food and history introduced to me years earlier. Destination: Siena, in the region of Tuscany.

I had booked a hotel that was central to the main piazza, within walking distance of most of the sites I had planned to visit. When I arrived, the elderly porter, who looked as if he had been there since the place had been built, helped me with my luggage. He was friendly. I was surprised that such a small family-run hotel could survive the economic crisis Italy was facing.

My cozy 'stanza' (as the Italians would call it), was located on the second floor. It was well-furnished and comfortable. An old ceiling fan made a humming sound as it rotated, moving the warm air around the room. Tired from the journey, I showered and got into bed earlier than usual, but was unable to fall asleep. I decided to open the window, only to find the evening air outside warmer than that in the room. I closed it, climbed back into bed, turned the old bedside lamp on and began reading a novel I had bought at the airport. The biography of an inspiring man, Nelson Mandela. A political leader who had overcome the impossible and lived to tell the tale.

I was not even halfway down the first page when the lamp flickered. I dismissed it as the quirks of old wiring. The air in the room became cooler and seemed to thicken, impacting on my ability to breathe. I looked up and in an attempt to expand my lungs, I breathed in deeply.

Then, I noticed him. A man, in his early twenties wearing a military uniform, was standing at the foot of the bed. His expression was sad, almost nostalgic. My skin turned ice cold. I did not move. His dark eyes were intense and remained fixed on me as he approached the edge of the bed, where he paused, then sat down. I felt the mattress depress as he sat and leaned forward to touch my hand, leaving me utterly petrified and paralyzed by a mixture of fear, sadness and empathy. It was a touch that was so cold, but at the same time gentle. Suddenly, as if by telepathy, I became aware of his name. Vincenzo. Then, as quietly as he had appeared, Vincenzo's essence dissipated.

While still transfixed and staring at the spot where he had rested, I became aware that during the visitation, I had been partially holding my breath, resulting in my feeling light headed. A few moments passed before my heart rate decreased as I consciously normalized my breathing. Alone again, I was left wondering about the young soldier's passing.

The following morning I was greeted by the manager who enquired if my night had been restful. I hesitated before answering.

"I didn't get much sleep. I kept on having strange dreams," was all I could volunteer.

"Come," he said, "I wish to share something with you."

I followed him into a small room behind the reception area, not knowing what to expect. Reaching for the top shelf of an antique cabinet, he pulled down and handed me a small portrait of a young couple on their wedding day. Instantly, I recognized the groom.

"Vincenzo was my Great Uncle. Before going to war," he explained, "he and his new bride honeymooned in this hotel and in the room you now occupy. He was killed at the front.

I was surprised at such a spontaneous and open revelation. The feeling of sadness in me returned. I wondered how hard it must have been for his young wife to lose her loved one so prematurely. Replacing the picture on the shelf I turned to speak, but found myself alone. The manager was nowhere. Gone. Returning to the front desk I was, for a second time that morning, greeted by a manager. A different and very much alive one.

I don't know why Vincenzo showed himself to me. Maybe I reminded him of his young bride or perhaps he just wanted to be remembered and his story told. I stayed on at the hotel, but never saw him again.

CHAPTER TWENTY-SIX

Moved by what he had just read, Max found himself reaching for his iPad and searching Google for the hotel portrayed in the anecdote. Hotel Murelli. Clicking onto the link he discovered that it had been a family-run business since the early 1900s, and indeed it was reported to be haunted.

Sightings of men in military uniform and poltergeist activity had also been described by historians and paranormal investigators. What Olivia had experienced at that place must have been unsettling, but it seemed benign compared to what Max was reading about other guests and their ghostly encounters. Feeling a sense of gratitude and satisfaction that he had been able to corroborate events Olivia had described, to honor her memory, Max decided to press on with her story. Before he could do so, his mobile phone vibrated. Max declined the call.

In a room down the hall, Sean lay in bed, not fully recovered from earlier events that evening. He turned on the television hoping to distract himself from his growing anxiety. Eventually he fell into a fitful sleep.

As Max read, he could hear the sound of the television coming from Sean's room. It was disrupting his concentration and dulling the enjoyment of being in the moment with Olivia's experiences. Irritated, he made his way to Sean's room preparing to reprimand him for being inconsiderate. After opening the door he could see that Sean had fallen asleep. He watched him for a moment before entering and switching off the large flat screen TV. Filled with a fleeting moment of tenderness, before exiting, he glanced back at him and whispered, "Good night, my boy."

The night's conditions were mild, graced with light winds and little humidity, making it conducive to having the windows open. Sitting comfortably in his large four-poster bed, in total privacy, Max began another chapter.

CHAPTER TWENTY-SEVEN

The sun shone through the open window into the master bedroom. Max had fallen asleep before closing it. Rays of bright warm sunlight caressed his face, gently easing him out of a deep slumber. He opened one eye to check the time on the clock sitting on the bedside table. Satisfied that it wasn't late, slowly and drearily Max sat up and rubbed away the sleep from his eyes.

Despite feeling drained of energy, he made his way into the bathroom to shower. The warm water did little to ease the undeniable emotional discomfort he was suffering. After drying himself, he looked at his reflection in the bathroom mirror, hating what he saw. It seemed as though in only a few days, he had aged by ten years. He rubbed his hand over the stubble on his chin, noticing all the emerging white hairs that, combined with his pale complexion, gave him an almost ghostly appearance. As he was about to reach for the electric shaver, he paused. Out of the corner of his eye Max caught a glimpse of something moving past the bathroom door.

"Sean?" he called out. No answer. Slowly he moved back into his bedroom, expecting to see his son borrowing his Armani cologne. The room was empty.

He sighed heavily, then returned to complete his routine of morning grooming.

Max couldn't shake the sensation of being watched as he dressed and made his way into the kitchen. Reaching the coffee machine, he stopped and averted his gaze to the wooden block in which an assortment of knives rested. He moved closer to it as if drawn in that direction by an irresistible force. Choosing one of the larger ones, while running his forefinger along its blade, Max contemplated his next move.

CHAPTER TWENTY-EIGHT

That night, Sean had slept poorly. The strain of his father's uncharacteristic behavior weighed heavily on him. Deciding to have breakfast before his father awoke, in order to avoid another confrontation, he showered quickly, then dressed, before hastily making his way into the kitchen. To his surprise, his father stood at the sink with his back to him. Perturbed by what he saw, he attempted to quietly back out. But Max, having seen Sean's reflection in the window, turned his head slightly and speaking to him from over his shoulder, invited him to have breakfast.

"Good morning, son." He said cheerfully, now turning to face him. "What can I get you?"

"Just a glass of OJ, thanks," Sean replied, glancing at the knife held firmly in his father's hand.

"How about some toast?" he asked with an atypical tone accompanying the fixed and strained smile, as he poured the juice.

"Sure," Sean replied, still watching the knife, as Max moved slowly and deliberately to hand him the chilled drink.

"Refreshing," Sean said after taking a few gulps. Max was still smiling.

Then, suddenly, the smile disappeared. The two men stood before one another, the rising tension in the room palpable. Sean mustered all the resilience he had in him to remain composed. Max was looking past him with an odd expression. The youth felt his skin, now clammy, begin to crawl, but didn't dare turn around, fearing how his father might react. Unexpectedly, Max dropped the knife onto the wooden floor, and slowly backing away from his son, retreated into the hallway.

Once again, Sean was left in shock. He felt light headed and nauseated, regurgitating the juice into the sink. After steadying himself, he thought about calling the police, but reconsidered, fearing that they wouldn't take him seriously, or worse, that they would have both of them locked up. Then it came to him. He knew who he could rely on. Removing his iPhone from his pocket, with urgency Sean texted a message.

CHAPTER TWENTY-NINE

The morning air was fresh. The birds sang their morning tunes filling the quaint garden with music, while the sun warmed the water in the small stone bird bath, occupied by a couple of sparrows. Max sat on the grass cross-legged next to a bed of roses in a far corner of the garden. The tranquility of nature contrasted with the psychological turmoil that he felt. The inability to explain the fluctuation in his mood and frequent dark thoughts made him question his sanity. He was tormented.

His thoughts drifted back to Olivia and her diary. Was this some kind of punishment for not helping her when he had the chance? He quickly dismissed the idea, recalling that she had indeed described him as 'a good clinician'. A fleeting sense of calm overcame him. Now he remembered how special he had felt, knowing Olivia had taken the time before her passing, to impart this very personal information. It couldn't have been to punish him, after all, he had helped her manage her anxiety. There had to be another purpose. But what? The answer was locked away somewhere in his subconscious mind. Would it ever be allowed to drift to the surface?

CHAPTER THIRTY

Pamela Stein awoke startled by the nightmare she'd just had. Sitting up and leaning against the bedhead in a hotel room far away from home, she struggled to catch her breath. Her tanned skin was moist with sweat, causing her nightgown to cling to her slender body. Glancing to her right, she saw her travel companion and best friend, Sally, still fast asleep. Grabbing her phone, she quietly made her way into their small en-suite bathroom and closed the door.

Looking at her wrist watch, Pamela calculated the three hour time difference. It would have been mid-morning in the Hamptons. But her iPhone displayed a low battery signal, only sufficient charge for the phone to ring a couple of times before it would die. Sitting on the cold tiled floor, Pamela reflected on the content of her dream. She was worried by the images of Sean being smothered by a pair of large hands reaching from behind, his eyes widening with terror and helplessness. Was he in danger? Who would want to harm him?

A gentle knock at the bathroom door interrupted her thoughts. It was Sally.

"Good morning," Sally greeted, peering into the bathroom from behind the door she had partially opened.

Puzzled by her friend's worried look, she joined Pamela, sitting next to her. "Are you ok?" she asked.

"Yeah, I just can't get hold of Max or Sean," she began, "and to make matters worse my phone needs a full recharge."

"That's easy, just use my charger."

"Thanks, Sally," Pamela said, getting to her feet and going back into their bedroom, not wanting her friend to notice her level of concern and press for an explanation. Instead, she said, "What about going to the Santa Lucia street market? I'd like to pick up a couple of t-shirts for Max and Sean."

"Great!" Sally replied, moving toward the basin to wash her face.

After a simple breakfast at the local coffee shop, the two women headed for the streets of Santiago.

As they approached the entrance, they could see that the market was bustling with business. Locals and tourists alike were bargaining at the stalls before committing to a deal. Despite still feeling uneasy about her son's safety, Pamela was intrigued and amused by the variety in the display of body language, some behaviors more subtle, while others more animated. Pamela noticed that it would usually be the locals who would gesticulate wildly. Holding an item they'd move closer to the prospective customer inviting them to feel a fabric, while the other party shrank back, gesturing with their hands indicating that they were not interested. It was just what she needed. A brief humorous distraction.

"Hey, Pam," Sally exclaimed, "here are some groovy t-shirts". Pam turned her attention to what she was being shown.

"Neat! They will love these patterns."

It didn't take her long to find the correct sizes. Opening her purse, she pulled out a handful of Pesos and without bargaining, handed the exact amount to the young lady manning the stall.

"Gracias," Pamela said, smiling, but before she turned to leave, an older woman with advanced cataracts in one eye, who had been perched on an old stool, stepped forward, blocking her way. Surprised by this, both Pamela and Sally looked to the younger lady for an explanation.

"*Mala onda! Mala onda!*" the old woman repeated while thrusting sticks of incense into Pamela's hand.

"She wants you to take those for protection. There is a bad feeling surrounding you," the younger lady explained. Hesitantly, Pamela accepted the sticks, placing them in the carrier bag.

Worried, and without delay, Pamela hurried back to their hotel to call home.

CHAPTER THIRTY-ONE

Sean observed his father from a safe distance, before stepping onto the lawn to approach him. Drawing closer, he watched for any sign of tension in Max's body language.

"Hey, Dad," Sean said as casually as he could, "Enjoying the sun?"

"Indeed. The sun, the roses, the birds. The beauty of nature," Max replied flatly.

"Well, I was thinking of playing mini golf this morning. Mom says you're pretty good at it. Maybe you can show me how to improve my game?" he suggested, hoping his father would accept the invitation.

"Ok," Max replied with a hint of enthusiasm. "What time did you have in mind?"

"I've booked us for around eleven."

"You've booked *us*?" his father asked, surprised.

"Yeah. Remember, Harvey said he was keen to have a game, the night we played Scrabble," Sean lied.

"Sure, son. I remember," Max answered keeping up his façade. He didn't remember, and it felt like there was a lot he didn't remember lately. "I'll do a bit of reading since there's still plenty of time."

Max got to his feet and walked back into the house. Sean sighed a sigh of relief, but was anxious about the ongoing obsession Max had with that diary.

CHAPTER THIRTY-TWO

My journey through Tuscany was pleasant, but like most good holidays was over too soon. On the flight home I was seated next to a cantankerous man who couldn't seem to get comfortable. His large frame and long legs were not suited for an economy seat in the middle aisle.

"Excuse me, Miss," he said, stopping one of the flight attendants walking down the gangway, "I am really uncomfortable here. I want to switch seats immediately!"

"Sir, the flight is full," she began, but was interrupted by his protests becoming louder and more threatening. "If you don't do something now, I am going to make sure you never fly again!"

The attendant remained composed and professional, promising that she would try to find a solution.

"Don't try, sweetheart. Just get it done!" the man sneered, using a condescending tone.

I couldn't help but feel sorry for her, so casually I insinuated that maybe in future, he should fly business class. He glared at me.

"Don't start with me. My lady says the same," he said, sulking like a petulant child. Moments later the attendant returned with good news. Someone had agreed to swap a seat located next to the emergency exit.

After agreeing to assist in the event of an emergency (as per the airline's policy), the two passengers made the switch.

"Hi, I'm Paul Tulli," the friendly good-looking young man said, extending his hand once he had stowed his carry-on bag. He sat down beside me.

"Olivia Croft," I replied smiling. "You're a life saver. I don't think I could have stood much longer sitting next to that man."

Paul grinned. His brown eyes, dark wavy hair and tanned skin was extremely easy on the eye.

We learned a lot about each other on that flight. We both lived in New York, came from supportive families and were ambitious. He loved to read, being an editor and publicist for a major publishing house, while I, being a newly graduated lawyer, loved to talk. We complemented each other perfectly. Once again I resorted to my old habit of touching him gently on the arm as we conversed. I had to make sure this pleasant experience was true and one of this world. It was. I relaxed.

Paul and I dated for almost eighteen months and then, after a brief engagement, we were married. On my wedding day, I thought that by the grace of mercy, the spirit world would not intrude on this special and very happy occasion. I was wrong.

I felt excited as I was getting dressed with the help of my bridesmaid, Ginger, in a room of the venue, where my fiancé and I would soon exchange vows. The dress I had chosen was simple in its design, with just enough lace making it elegant. The tiara decorated with small beads rested firmly on my crown.

"The veil is in the other room," Ginger remarked. "Don't move, I'll be right back," she said, leaving me standing in front of the gold plated full length mirror.

A few moments passed. I was admiring my side profile in the mirror when I noticed in the reflection the door behind me opening, until it was wide enough for someone to enter. Nobody did. Then, it forcefully slammed shut. I stood perfectly still, waiting for what was to come next. Turning my head slightly, I wondered if something more discernible would manifest. Nothing. The temperature in the room dropped, leading the air to become charged with an indescribable negative energy. I waited. All my senses were on 'high alert'. Still nothing. Then the door opened again. Ginger entered, carefully and tenderly holding my veil.

"Jeez! What are they doing with the air conditioning? It's freezing!" she remarked, shivering slightly.

I was aware that we were in the company of something sinister and feared that it could possibly attach itself to one of us, so I urged Ginger to finalize the fitting in another room. Would this have made a difference, having learned about spirits and their ability to travel through space? Probably not, but this time, it was my way of taking control of the uninvited.

CHAPTER THIRTY-THREE

Max sat on his bed, and for a brief moment felt at peace. His thoughts returned to the recently read description of Olivia's encounter with her future husband. It made him smile. There were similarities in her story to his first meeting with Pamela.

They had met in almost identical circumstances twenty years earlier. Both he and Pam had been traveling home from Europe. Pamela had swapped seats to accommodate a larger gentleman only to be seated next to Max. She was a consultant for a Microsoft company, with a keen sense of adventure, a wicked sense of humor and a holistic approach to life. He reminisced about their first date, where to impress her he had taken her skydiving. More memories flooded his consciousness.

Their wedding day. The small chapel, where in an intimate ceremony, they had exchanged vows. A feeling of tenderness overcame him as he recalled. She had looked beautiful in her wedding gown, her hair styled so that it could support the small tiara and veil. The reception had been held at their cottage, in this very garden. So many loving and joyous memories warmed his heart, like the time Pam had informed him that she was expecting a baby. The first time he had cradled Sean in his arms.

Sean's first step and first word. Then, an interesting but long-forgotten memory emerged from the depths of his being. Sean would have been four years old, when as a family, they had vacationed in Mexico, enjoying the summer at a little beach resort in Acapulco. Neither he nor Pamela spoke any Spanish at the time, but little Sean seemed to have picked up quite a few words.

"My friend Pablo taught me how to say 'hello,'" little Sean had stated enthusiastically. There were no other children at the resort, nor had they seen any kids play with him. At the time he and Pamela were amused, thinking that their son had an imaginary friend. Now it made Max even more curious about his son's 'friend', Pablo. Was he a child ghost? Had Sean, like Olivia, experienced the paranormal? Had he had any other encounters? Had they been frightening? So many questions to be answered.

Then, sadness announced itself, clouding his soul and jolting him back to the present.

"Dad, I'm good to go," Sean called out from the foyer. Max closed the diary, and forcing a smile for the occasion, grabbed his keys off the night table and went downstairs to join his son.

Ironically, being a therapist himself, he was aware with each passing day of becoming more overwhelmed by and less in control of his feelings. The possibility of becoming unhinged unnerved Max, but the potential consequence frightened him even more.

CHAPTER THIRTY-FOUR

As they arrived at the club house, Sean spotted Harvey buying a cold drink from the vending machine.

Relieved that now he had the support of a trusted friend, Sean called out to him.

"Hey, Harvey!"

The older man looked in their direction and waved.

"Sean. Max," he said, greeting them each with a manly hug.

"I'll get the equipment from the rentals counter," Max said, moving away from his partners.

"Thanks for coming. I didn't know who else to call," Sean confessed once his father was out of earshot.

"He doesn't look half bad to me," Harvey observed. "You, on the other hand, look terrible."

"His mood swings are just unpredictable," Sean began, but was interrupted by Max returning with their gear in tow. He was smiling and seemed to have a spring in his step. Sean, however, was unnerved.

****

The game of mini golf proved just what Sean and Max needed. Although of late their relationship had been strained, it seemed to Sean that Max seemed more relaxed and to be genuinely enjoying the outing. After the game Harvey offered to take his friends to lunch, but Sean had made other plans. So had Max. Sean opted to get a drink of water from a nearby fountain while his father returned the hired equipment. Sean's phone buzzed. Looking at the screen, he read a message from Harvey.

"Call me anytime if you need help," Max was fast approaching. Unable to reply without his father noticing, he replaced device in his pocket.

"You beat me again," Sean stated, trying to convey admiration.

"Oh, well, son. I had a bit more practice than you. Your mother and I used to play a lot. It was she who taught me those little tricks."

"Yeah, right," the youth replied teasingly.

"What are your plans for the rest of the day?" he enquired as they walked to the Jeep.

"I was going to ask if I could spend the night at George's. He and some friends are doing a horror movie marathon," he explained. Max considered his own options. More time to read seemed appealing.

"Fine by me," he replied in an unusually cheerful tone. Sean picked up on the enthusiasm, unsure what to make of it. Before being able to say anything further, his mobile phone rang. It was his mother.

"Hey, Mom," he said casually.

"Honey, is everything ok? I was worried when I couldn't get hold of anyone at the house, and your father isn't answering his cell phone," she explained. Sean looked at his father who now was starting the engine and backing out of the parking bay.

"Yeah Mom, we are fine," he replied with hesitancy in his tone.

"Oh, thank God! How's your father?" she asked.

Sean paused a moment before answering, "He's ok." More silence across the line.

"I'm worried, honey. I've changed my ticket to come home early. I'm leaving in a couple of hours," she announced. Sean was relieved, but couldn't convey this without the risk of triggering another of his father's dark moods.

"Sounds good. I've got to go mom, I'll speak to you later." After ending the call Sean wondered why his father had been ignoring calls and even more curious, was why he hadn't enquired about the woman he loved who, had just been on the phone. Sean was disturbed by the lack of interest. They drove home in silence.

After the call had ended, Pamela was convinced that she was making the right decision.

CHAPTER THIRTY-FIVE

Sean had gone to his friend's place. Max was alone, or so he thought. The air in the home was cool but the air conditioned room felt cooler than the temperature that had been pre-programmed. He looked for the diary in his bedroom, which was where he had left it earlier that day. It wasn't there. Methodically Max searched the entire cottage before finally finding it in the study next to his computer. Uncertain as to how it had got there, but relieved to have found it, he gently picked it up. Feeling its soft leather cover soothed him. He closed his eyes to savor the moment.

Then, suddenly a noise. "**BLIPP**!" Opening his eyes, Max found that the computer had turned itself on and was running through its usual software safety checks. Max froze.

The screen opened up to the Google search page. He waited. His heart and breath rate quickening. Then, still unbelieving, he watched each key move of their own accord spelling R-O-S-E, followed by T-H-A-M-A-L-I. The cursor then flew across the screen to the 'Enter' icon.

He waited, feeling the blood drain from his face. A website of a clairvoyant appeared. Unable to move, with every fiber in his body feeling stiff, he was paralyzed by the terror of the unimaginable.

The moment was interrupted by the ring tone of his mobile phone. The jolly and upbeat music by Bob Sinclair almost made him jump out of his skin. Max reacted quickly by reaching into his pocket to answer it. His hands trembled so badly, that he dropped the device. Once he had retrieved the phone, still filled with apprehension, he accepted the call.

"Dr. Maxwell Stein?" the unfamiliar female voice enquired.

"Speaking," he answered, masking his inner tension.

"Don't be alarmed. My name is Rose Thamali," she said, before continuing, "you are probably wondering how I got your number."

"Well, of course," Max answered, intimidated, staring at the name on the computer screen hoping there would be a simple and logical explanation. A pause.

"I'm a clairvoyant," she began, "Olivia has contacted me." More silence on Max's part. "She wants me to tell you that she is pleased you've been reading her diary. Continue reading it."

Consumed with tension from the fear, Max wanted to break down and cry, but couldn't. Something forced him to stay strong. He was speechless. To his relief the psychic continued talking.

"Olivia's spirit is attached to you. You've helped her in life for which she is grateful. Now it's her turn to help you," she said.

"Help me with what?" he asked, confused and now more than ever, fearing he was slipping away from the verge of sanity.

"Tell me, damn it!" he almost shouted, sensing the psychic's hesitation to impart pertinent information.

"Fear not Dr. Stein, everything is going to be just fine," were the last words from the stranger's mouth. Max wasn't convinced or reassured by her prediction. At that moment, he felt intensely panicked about his son's future. The vision of Sean a few nights earlier once again flashed into his mind. Frantic about Sean's safety, he called him.

****

Hearing his son's voice over the phone was the best thing that had happened to Max since starting their vacation together. In spite of learning that Sean was in good and safe company, he cautioned him to drive carefully on his way home in the morning. Tired and somewhat reluctant, he felt obliged to pick up the diary and continue reading. His head throbbed. Max swallowed a couple of aspirin and washed them down with a gulp from the bottle of Scotch left on the table. If he was going to be able to concentrate he needed to fight off a full-blown migraine from developing. In truth he didn't know how much fight he had left in him. He began to read.

****

One thing I've figured out, is that when we are born our destiny is already mapped out for us by a higher power. Being of Christian faith, for me that higher power is God, for you it might be something different. This morning my grandfather paid me a visit, in spirit form of course. His message is simple: "You haven't much time left. Resolve any unfinished business while you still can." I am not afraid. I know exactly what he means and what I need to do."

The writing stopped. There were no more entries, yet Max noted the diary still had several blank pages left. He felt disappointed with a sense of emptiness that there was no more to be told. Then he thought back to that Saturday morning. He *had* been told the full story. He himself had read the article covering her tragic death in the newspaper. He felt exhausted, but also vindicated, that she had told him her story and that he had been able to appreciate the intensity of her experiences. Feeling physically and emotionally drained, Max made himself comfortable on the couch, allowing himself to drift off for an afternoon nap.

CHAPTER THIRTY-SIX

Upon waking, Max was unsure of how much time had passed. Glancing at his wrist watch he noted that several hours had lapsed. He stood up, seeing from the muted light in the garden, that the sun had gone down and nightfall was approaching. Looking at his desk where the diary had been left, he saw that it was no longer there. A moment of longing and restlessness traveled through his body. Scanning the room with a sense of urgency, he finally found it sitting on the top shelf of the book case. 'Who had placed it there,' he wondered.

Suddenly, he heard voices. Surprised, he entered the kitchen only to be surrounded by familiar faces. His wife Pamela, Sean, Harvey and Shirley. They were crying. Confused and with initial indecision he edged forward. Then to his horror he saw paramedics walk out of the cottage. They were carrying a stretcher. A chilling feeling of dread smothered him, coupled with a sense of psychological disconnect from his surroundings.

Desperately he tried to get someone's attention. Now with urgency rising within him, Max was shouting at the top of his lungs. "Hey! I'm here! What's going on?" It was useless. He was being ignored. Nobody could hear or see him. Then looking back to where he had been resting and spotting the resuscitation equipment being stowed by an ambulance officer, he understood.

He had just died.

A form approached him from behind. Turning, he saw her. Olivia. She smiled but was silent. Gently taking him by the hand, she guided him through the open patio door and into another world.

Printed in the USA
CPSIA information can be obtained
at www.ICGtesting.com
LVHW081748031123
762986LV00046B/1078